Text and illustrations copyright © 2006 Stairway Publications

Published by Stairway Publications
PO Box 518
Huntington, NY 11743-0518
USA

Visit us at: www.stairwaypub.com

ISBN-10: 0-9740061-1-4

ISBN-13: 978-0-9740061-1-6

LCCN 2005902403

First edition 2006

Printed in Hong Kong

Written by
Madeline Arroyo

Illustrated by
S. Dean Vavak

Huntington, New York

The morning sun was warm on his face as Matthias made his way to his father's shop. One left turn and then another.

As he entered the shop he could hear the potter's wheel already spinning. The boy made his way to his work area and sat down. The workday had begun.

"Careful, Son," his father warned. "Don't squeeze too hard. We don't want any dents in our water jar, now do we?"

"No, Papa!" Matthias responded, and relaxed his small fingers over the spinning clay. "This is going to be the most beautiful water jar at Jacob's wedding."

"That's the spirit," his father praised. "Make a jar worthy of the future best potter in all of Bethlehem!"

Matthias smiled and glided his fingers gently over the wet clay. Someday he *would* be a master potter, like his father.

"No
dar

"Th
Go
You

The

his

When he could, Matthias loved playing hide-and-seek with his friends. But as winter approached, the days grew shorter. His friends would play fewer rounds of the game.

The whole family had just sat down to dinner when Matthias announced that he could hear footsteps approaching from outside. Within moments there was a knock on the door.

"Come in, friend," his father called out from his seat.

The man who came through the doorway was a stranger. Matthias had never heard his voice before.

"Forgive me for interrupting your dinner," the man apologized. "Maybe you've heard the news," he said. "Strange things have taken place. They're being talked about throughout the town."

"What things?" Papa asked. "Forgive me, but I've never seen you before. Where have you come from?"

"I know the way to Thaddeus's inn," Matthias said. "It's at the far end of town. And I can find his stable. I know where it is by the smell of the animals."

The man was overjoyed. Turning to Matthias's father he said, "Please, I would be glad to give the boy a coin for his time."

"Yes Papa," Matthias begged. "Let me take the man to the stable and the special baby!"

"Well." His father hesitated, looking at his wife. "I suppose it will be alright. Matthias can find his way in the dark as easily as at midday. Go in peace," he said to the stranger.

Matthias leaped from the table, thrilled at the new adventure. Stretching out his traveling stick, he made his way quickly to the door.

It was a long walk, but Matthias found his way easily. As they walked across the quiet town, the man shared all he'd heard about the baby, whose birth angels had announced.

"There it is, Matthias. I can see the stable from here!" The stranger took Matthias by the arm and hurried him along.

Once in the stable, the man released the boy's arm and moved quietly away. Matthias could sense that there were several people in the stable, yet no one spoke a word. He wasn't sure what he should do. In the quiet he could hear the sounds of the infant.

"May I touch the baby?" he asked.

"Of course you may, but you must be very gentle." The voice was that of a young woman.

A man's arm went around Matthias's shoulder and gently led him to where the baby lay.

"Give me your hand," the woman said. Taking the boy's hand, she laid it on the baby's hand.

Matthias held the soft, tiny hand. The angel had said that this was a Savior. His own hand was so much bigger than the baby's. Yet in the baby's touch he sensed a strength that filled him with wonder. And Matthias believed the angel's words.

Thirty winters came and went, but Matthias never forgot that night, or the special baby. He was now a master potter, the best in all of Bethlehem. Yet even though his life was happy and full, his heart was always searching. What he was looking for, he didn't know.

One afternoon as he was making deliveries, Matthias heard the sound of many voices and running feet. He pulled his donkey close to him and held the animal's harness as he listened.

People were gathering from every direction. When people came near, he asked what was happening.

Jacob the tailor answered, "A young carpenter and rabbi named Jesus of Nazareth is coming down the street."

The sounds of the crowd were drawing closer.

"Many believe this man is the Messiah God promised us.
They say he heals cripples and gives sight to the blind."

Jacob grabbed Matthias's shoulders.

"Matthias, this man raises the dead!"

Jacob suddenly released him and turned away.

"He's here." Jacob's voice faded as he quickly walked away to
get a better look at Jesus.

Matthias's heart leaped within him for joy. He had been in the presence of the Messiah once before. But his joy turned to confusion as he realized that the crowd was coming directly toward him.

As they got closer to him, the crowd grew silent. Matthias found it hard to stand as he felt a power around him he had never felt before. One person drew near him.

"Matthias, salvation has come to you this day." As the man spoke he put his hands on the potter's head.

An almost unbearable current of heat coursed through Matthias's body. What was happening? Strange shapes were forming in his head. And suddenly his eyes started to blink as his eyes awakened to the sunlight.

"He can see!" a man shouted.

Matthias's body trembled with emotion. People were all around him, some praising God and some crying. His eyes focused their new sight on the young face before him.

In the eyes that looked at him, Matthias recognized the same gentleness and strength that he had experienced in the touch of a tiny hand so many years ago.

"Lord," he said, putting out his arms and falling upon Jesus' chest, "I found you."

"Matthias," Jesus answered as His arms embraced the little potter, "I found *you*."

Dedication

Madeline Arroyo dedicates this book to:

Angela Patanio, for her heart to share the love of Jesus Christ with the physically challenged. Thank you for your friendship.

-Madeline

Dean Vavak dedicates this book to:

My children, without you I would have had a very empty (and boring) life. Thank you Christopher Stephen, Mari Emily, Jonathan Ewan, Joseph Peter, Elizabeth Jane, Michelle Cassidy and Daniel Zachary. And I thank God for each of your special gifts.

- Dad

Other children's books by Madeline Arroyo:

Calie's Gift
Illustrated by S. Dean Vavak
ISBN 0-9740061-0-6